SEE HOW THEY GROW

MOUSE

photographed by
BARRIE WATTS

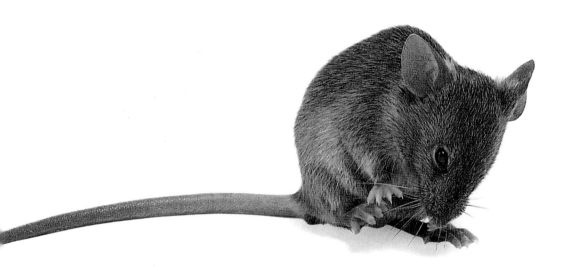

Lodestar Books • Dutton • New York

Just arrived

I have just been born.
I cannot see or hear.
I have no fur to
keep me warm.

I snuggle in a
cozy nest with my
brothers and sisters.

This is me

This is our mother. She is
coming to feed us her milk.
We are very hungry.

Out of the nest

I am two days old. Fine black
hair is growing over my pink skin.
My eyes and ears are still closed.

Where am I?
I am lost!

I squeak as loud as I can so Mother hears me. She will carry me home.

My first crawl

I am two weeks old. My eyes
are open. At last I can see
and hear. I can walk too.

My mother watches me explore.
I sniff everything I find.

Now I am going back to my nest for a nap. It has been an exciting day.

Looking after ourselves

Now I am four weeks old.
I spend most of the
time with my brothers and sisters.

We play together.

Then I clean
myself. My
long tail needs
special care.

Climbing high

I am six weeks old.
My brothers, sisters,
and I have climbed
this branch.

We cling to the thin branches with our claws.

Our long tails help us to balance.

17

Finding food

Now I am eight
weeks old. I enjoy finding
my own food.

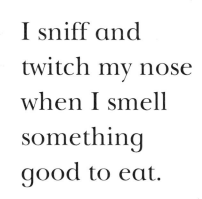

I sniff and
twitch my nose
when I smell
something
good to eat.

My favorite food
is grain. I hold
it between my
paws and nibble
it with my long
front teeth.

See how I grew

Newborn

Two days old

Two weeks old   Three weeks old   Four weeks old

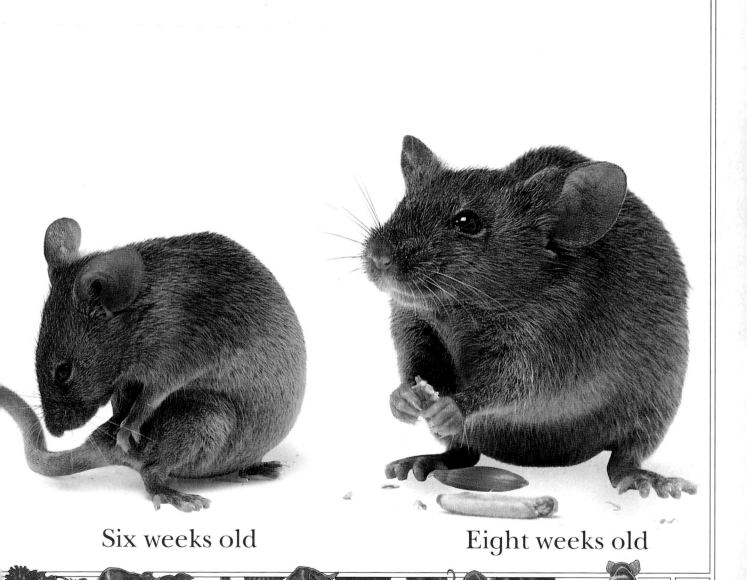

Six weeks old

Eight weeks old

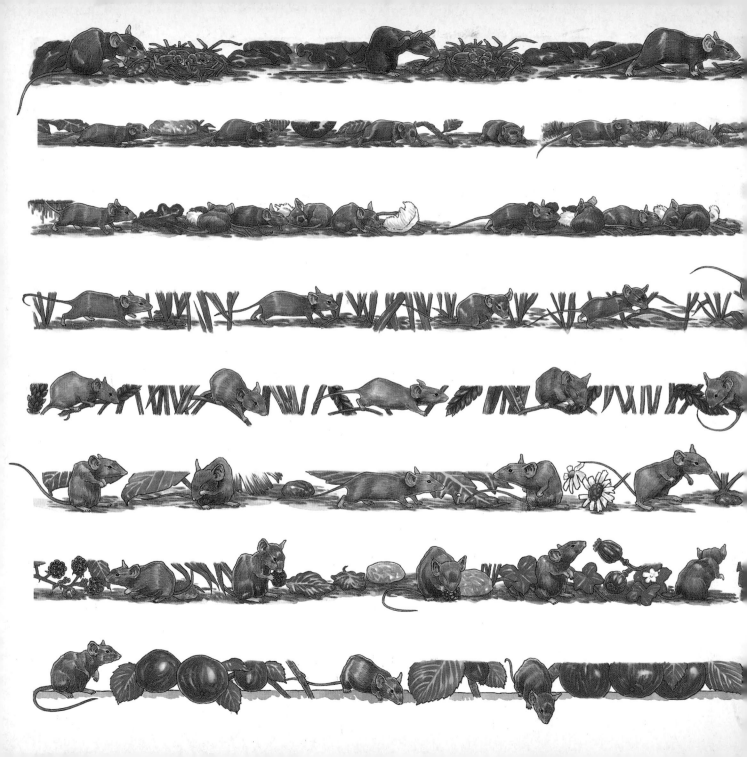